Can I Help?

by Marilyn Janovitz

North-South Books

New York | London

Copyright © 1996 by Marilyn Janovitz
Reprinted by permission of North-South Books Inc.
All rights reserved. No part of this book may be reproduced
or utilized in any form or by any means, electronic or mechanical,
including photocopying, recording, or any information storage
and retrieval system, without permission in writing from the publisher.

Published in the United States by North-South Books Inc., New York.

Published simultaneously in Great Britain, Canada, Australia, and
New Zealand in 1996 by North-South Books, an imprint of
Nord-Süd Verlag AG, Gossau Zürich, Switzerland.
First paperback edition published in 1998.

Library of Congress Cataloging-in-Publication Data.
Janovitz, Marilyn.
Can I help? / by Marilyn Janovitz.
Summary: A little wolf's father gratefully accepts his son's offer to work with him in
the garden, even though the cub is sometimes more of a hindrance than a help.
[1. Helpfulness—Fiction. 2. Gardening—Fiction. 3. Fathers and sons—Fiction.
4. Wolves—Fiction. 5. Stories in rhyme.] I. Title.
PZ8.3.J263Can 1996
[E]—dc20 95-36185
A CIP catalogue record for this book is available from The British Library.

The illustrations in this book were created
with colored pencil and watercolor.
Designed by Marc Cheshire

ISBN 1-55858-575-3 (TRADE BINDING)
1 3 5 7 9 TB 10 8 6 4 2
ISBN 1-55858-576-1 (LIBRARY BINDING)
1 3 5 7 9 LB 10 8 6 4 2
ISBN 1-55858-904-X (PAPERBACK)
1 3 5 7 9 PB 10 8 6 4 2
Printed in the United States of America

Can I help you do the mowing?

Yes, please help me do the mowing.

Can I help you with the hoeing?

Yes, please help me with the hoeing.

Do the mowing, help with hoeing.

Can I help you pull the weeds?

Yes, please help me pull the weeds.

Can I help you plant the seeds?

Yes, please help me plant the seeds.

Pull the weeds, plant the seeds,
Do the mowing, help with hoeing.

Can I help you fill the bath?

Yes, please help me fill the bath.

Can I help you sweep the path?

Yes, please help me sweep the path.

Fill the bath, sweep the path,
Pull the weeds, plant the seeds,
Do the mowing, help with hoeing.

Can I help you lift the pail?

Yes, please help me lift the pail.

Can I help you wrap your tail?

Yes, please help me wrap my tail.

Lift the pail, wrap your tail.
Fill the bath, sweep the path,
Pull the weeds, plant the seeds,
Do the mowing, help with hoeing.

Can I help you squirt the hose?

Yes, please help me squirt the hose.

Can I help you dry your nose?

Yes, please help me dry my nose.

Squirt the hose, dry your nose,
Lift the pail, wrap your tail
Fill the bath, sweep the path,
Pull the weeds, plant the seeds,
Do the mowing, help with hoeing.

Can I climb up on your lap?

Yes, please climb up on my lap.

We've worked hard, let's take a nap!